My Pet Turtle

by Deborah Reber
illustrated by David Cutting

SCHOLASTIC INC.
New York Toronto London Auckland Sydney
Mexico City New Delhi Hong Kong Buenos Aires

To my wonderful dog and forever puppy, Ari.—D. R.

For my Uncle, Henry Seegitz, whose influence
I could not have done without.—D. C.

Based on the TV series *Blue's Clues*® created by Traci Paige Johnson,
Todd Kessler, and Angela C. Santomero as seen on Nick Jr.®
On *Blue's Clues,* Steve is played by Steven Burns.

ISBN 0-439-35639-3

12 11 10 9 8 7 6 5 4 3 2 1   1 2 3 4 5 6/0

Printed in the U.S.A.

First Scholastic printing, September 2001

Hello! I am .
BLUE
Have you met my
pet , Turquoise?
TURTLE

Turquoise was a birthday 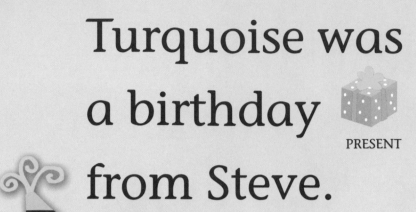 PRESENT from Steve.

He gave me the 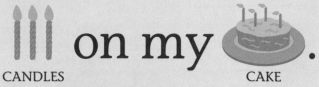 PRESENT
after I blew out the
CANDLES on my CAKE.

Inside the  PRESENT was my TURTLE , Turquoise! She smiled at me. I knew we would be friends!

My  TURTLE , Turquoise, lives in my bedroom.

She stays on the  TABLE
next to my 🛏 BED.

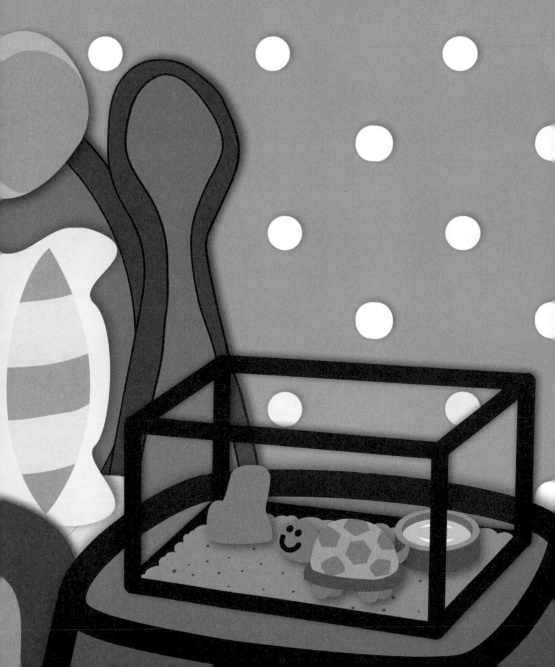

My 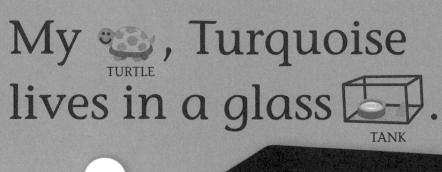 TURTLE, Turquoise lives in a glass  TANK.

She has sand and
a rock in her .

TANK

I take care of my , TURTLE
Turquoise, by feeding
her every morning.

She likes to eat 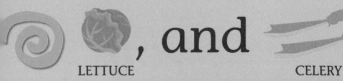,

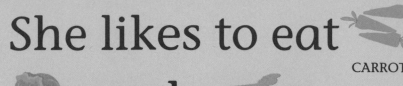, and .

CARROTS

LETTUCE   CELERY

My  , Turquoise,
TURTLE
needs 💧 to drink.
WATER

Every day I put fresh 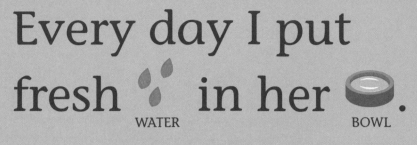 in her .

WATER

BOWL

One day we had
show-and-tell at .

SCHOOL

I brought my  in a glass to show my friends!

TURTLE

BOWL

Turquoise sat on my desk in her glass !

BOWL

She liked  very much.

much.

Sometimes my ,
TURTLE
Turquoise, sits with
me on the .
GRASS
She loves the .
SUN
It makes her happy.

When it is time to go to  **BED** we read a  **BOOK** together.

Turquoise loves to read with me.

I love my  ,
TURTLE
Turquoise! She is
a great pet and
a very good friend.